D0806792

STAR WARS®

CLONE WARS

ADVENTURES

VOLUME 3

designers
Lani Schreibstein & Josh Elliott

assistant editor
Dave Marshall

editor
Jeremy Barlow

publisher
Mike Richardson

special thanks to Sue Rostoni and Amy Gary
at Lucas Licensing

⟡ The events in this story take place approximately
six months after the Battle of Geonosis.

www.titanbooks.com
www.starwars.com

STAR WARS: CLONE WARS ADVENTURES volume 3, March 2005. Published by Titan Books, a division of Titan Publishing Group Ltd., 144 Southwark Street, London SE1 0UP. Star Wars ©2004 Lucasfilm Ltd. & ™. All rights reserved. Used under authorization. Text and illustrations for Star Wars are © 2005 Lucasfilm Ltd. No portion of this publication may be reproduced or transmitted, in any form or by any means, without the express written permission of the copyright holder, Inc. Names, characters, places, and incidents featured in this publication either are the product of the author's imagination or are used fictitiously. Any resemblance to actual persons (living or dead), events, institutions, or locales, without satiric intent, is coincidental. PRINTED IN ITALY

4 6 8 10 9 7 5

STAR WARS®

CLONE WARS
ADVENTURES
VOLUME 3

"ROGUES GALLERY"
script **Haden Blackman**
art **The Fillbach Brothers**
colors **Sigmund Torre**

"THE PACKAGE"
script **Ryan Kaufman**
art **The Fillbach Brothers**
colors **Pamela Rambo**

"STRANGER IN TOWN"
script and art **The Fillbach Brothers**
colors **Sno Cone Studios**

"ONE BATTLE"
script **Tim Mucci**
art **The Fillbach Brothers**
colors **Sigmund Torre**

lettering
Michael David Thomas

cover
The Fillbach Brothers and Dan Jackson

GUHHH...

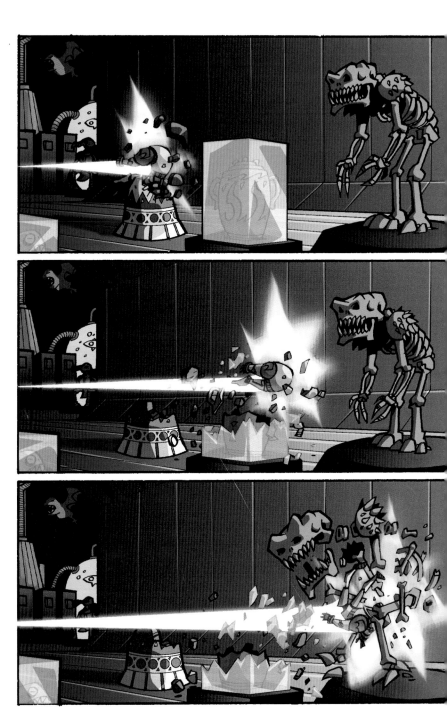

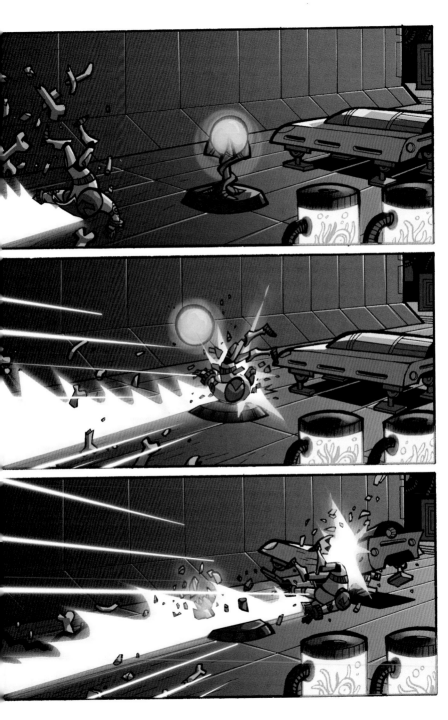

HE'S *FAST*, I'LL GIVE HIM THAT.

HE'S GONE AGAIN...

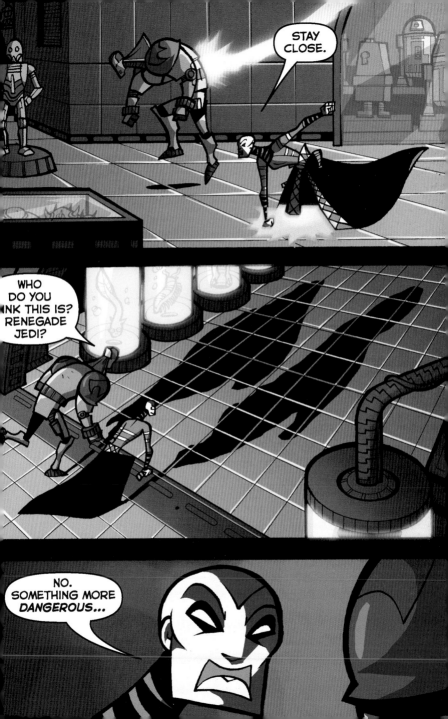

AAAAGH!

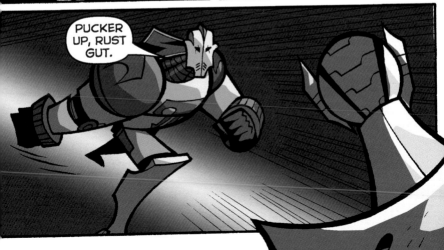

PUCKER UP, RUST GUT.

KLICK!

WHIRR!

VVMMM!

VVMMM!

WHO --

ARE --

YOU!?!

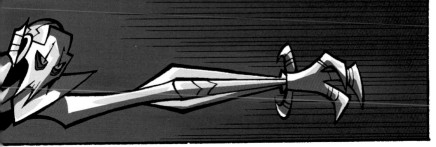

STAR WARS®

CLONE WARS
ADVENTURES
VOLUME 3

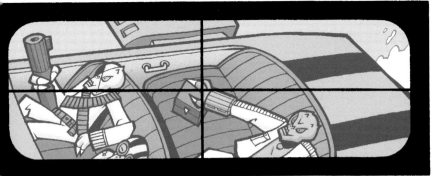

I SEE THE PACKAGE. SECOND SPEEDER.

GOOD. NOW WE THIN THE RANKS.

THWIP!

OOOF!

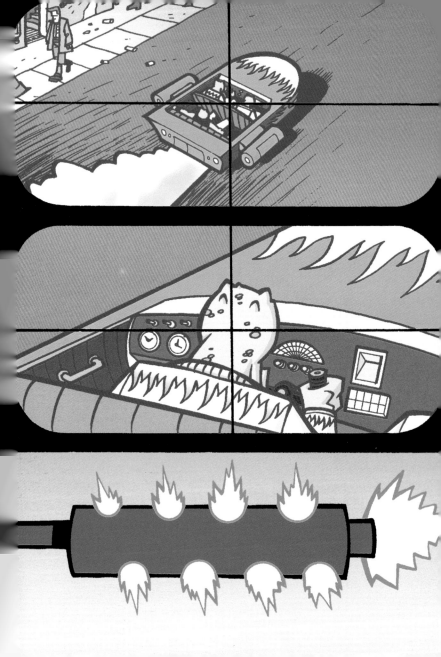

FAN OUT. SEARCH AND REPORT.

FIRE IN THE HOLE!

BZZZAAT!

BDEW!

BDEW!

BDEW!

BDEW!

BDEW!

TICK!

<<FIERFEK!>>

BA-BOOM

FWCOM!

BOOM!

AH...
NO...

STAR WARS®

CLONE WARS

ADVENTURES

VOLUME 3

WHAT'S IN THE BOX, LITTLE GUY?

CRUNGE!

DON'T PAY THEM NO NEVER MIND.

FOLKS 'ROUND HERE JUST DON'T TAKE TOO KINDLY TO STRANGERS...

...ESPECIALLY SINCE THEM SEPARATISTS HAVE COME ALONG AND STARTED TAKING OVER EVERY-THING.

GREETINGS CITIZENS.

WE HAVE COME TO CONFISCATE YOUR LAND.

THUP!

:GULP!:

STAR WARS®

CLONE WARS
ADVENTURES
VOLUME 3

BRACE FOR IMPACT!

KRA-THOOM!

DON'T WAIT FOR THE SMOKE TO CLEAR -- SEND THEM TO THE TRASH COMPACTORS!

COMMANDER!

"WE'RE IN TROUBLE!"

SURRENDER!

WE HAVE INCOMING.

WE'VE HELD OUT AS LONG AS WE COULD.

OUR REQUESTS FOR REINFORCEMENTS WERE CUT-OFF.

|||ᗐ/ᗐ ᗐᔕᛕ|ᔕᐯ||ᔔ ᗺᔕᏋᐯ|| ᗐᔕᎫᔕᏟI4ᔕᐢ:

SIR? I DON'T UNDERSTAND...

ᏟᔕᏅ Ꭻᔕ ᗐᏰ ᎫᗐᏃ ᗐ: Ꭻ:ᏟᔕᎫ ᐯᏟᔕᎫᎫᎫᏃᏟ: ᐯ||:+Ꮓ:

YES, SIR!

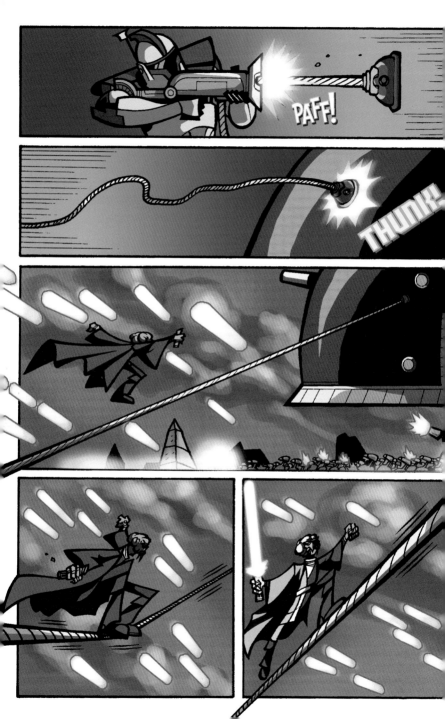

DOWN!!

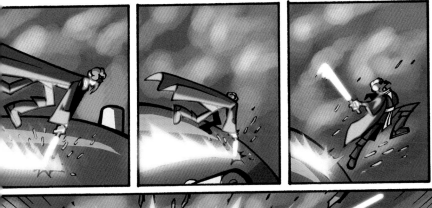

ᗞᗅᑯ ᑉᐊᒍᒣᒣᑐᒣ: ᗞᗅᑯ ᗴᑭᗴᑲ:

WHAT DID HE SAY, SIR?

HIM...? HE SAID...

"... ONE BATTLE, ONE JEDI."

THE END

STAR WARS
THE VIDEO GAME

RELEASING **APRIL 2005**

"IMPRESSIVE"
– IGN –

"ONE OF THE MOST VISUALLY STRIKING GAMES WE'VE SEEN"
– XBN –

All the characters, all the action, ALL THE FUN!

Play over 30 of your favorite characters, from Anakin to Yoda

Battle your way through Episodes I, II & III

Use the power of The Force

DOWNLOAD A **FREE DEMO** OF THE PC GAME AT
www.LEGOStarWarsTheVideoGame.com